T0365612

The Princess of Topaz
An African American Saga

Stella M. Reese

Order this book online at www.trafford.com
or email orders@trafford.com

Most Trafford titles are also available at major online book retailers.

Print information available on the last page.

Illustrators:	Book inspired by:	Special Thanks to:
Jessica L. Cheely	Charlotte B. Odusanya	My husband, Louis &
Melissa A. Cheely		The Gravley's

ISBN: 978-1-4269-2432-3 (sc)
       978-1-4669-2567-0 (e)

Library of Congress Control Number: 2009913213

Our mission is to efficiently provide the world's finest, most comprehensive book publishing service, enabling every author to experience success. To find out how to publish your book, your way, and have it available worldwide, visit us online at www.trafford.com

Trafford rev. 06/14/2021

www.trafford.com

North America & international
toll-free: 1 888 232 4444 (USA & Canada)
fax: 812 355 4082

I was standing on the porch of our old four room house which was painted grey; calling my dog. "Tag, it's time to eat." Tag is a mixed breed medium size brown dog. Tag rushes from the forest towards me and waits until I fill his bowl with tablescraps from our supper.

Tag plays and then eats. Afterwards, he retreats to his place underneath the house where he chose to make his own space.

Savannah feeding her dog

My name is Savannah. I am an African American girl with brown skin and black thick hair which is worn in braids. I wear patterned cotton dresses with ankle socks and brown oxford shoes. It is 1948. I live in Big Rock Virginia. I have a brother named Samuel. He looks like our father except a little heavier. He wears overalls most of the time, except for on Sundays when we all wear our "Sunday" clothes to church.

My Father, Alonzo is a coal miner. He is a tall, thin, brown skinned man who also usually wears overalls when not in his work gear.

Coal mine

We are poor but very happy and loved.
When Dad and the miners come from the mines underground, they are full of black coal dust.

They use the coal to burn in our stoves for cooking and heating. The coal is shipped all over the United States for the same purposes.

My father told me that he likes being a coal miner. After work, my father and brother play ball and do chores together. They also plant seeds for our flower and vegetable garden along with my mother.

Father and son playing ball/mother gardening

My father and brother cut wood in order for the fire to start in the stoves before adding the coal.

My brother and I love when our mother, Lotta comes home from work. She tells us about her work as a house maid. She is very beautiful. She is of medium height and weight and has brown smooth skin and shoulder length black hair which she wears in a bun as she wears her plain cotton dress. She puts on an apron and I help her cook supper. We usually have beans or greens seasoned with salt pork along with corn bread and fried chicken.

We slice fresh tomatoes and onions as a side dish. I love helping to make the fresh lemonade and the banana pudding for dessert.

Mother and daughter cooking

My mother and I talk a lot. I told her that I wanted to be a princess some day. She smiled and said, "Baby doll, you're already our little princess." I said, "thank you mama."

In the 1950's the schools were separated by race. I went to school in a 3 room schoolhouse with all of the other African American children. We were taught to read, write and do mathematics. We learned history but the only thing that we learned about ourselves was that our forefathers were slaves. I thought "Oh dear, I'm glad that we are not slaves anymore! I'm going to be a princess!"

School house with children and flag in yard

I grew up and graduated from high school and went to college in Bellevue, England in the late 50's as an exchange student on an academic scholarship.

I met a young student there who was tall, dark and handsome. He was also an exchange student from the country of Topaz. I learned that he was the only son of the king and queen of Topaz. His name was Frederick. He had an interest in me.

He would always smile and say, "hello" when he saw me. I would always blush and speak back. I also had an interest in him.

Couple standing on the college campus

Prince Frederick and I finally started to date. We fell in love. I flew with him to his home during school vacation to meet his parents.

Airplane flight

They liked me and also approved of me and soon Frederick and I became engaged to be married.

Our beautiful wedding was held on a lovely island in Southern Topaz. It was attended by many people from the island as well as my family and friends from Virginia and other states.

I chose our wedding theme to be topaz, the golden jewel which has the same name as Frederick's country. All of our wedding decorations encompassed the jewel, including the flowers.

My stunning dress and veil were white and my jewelry was gorgeous topaz.

My dream and wishes had come true! On that unforgettable day I became "The Princess of Topaz" and we lived a very happy life.

Wedding scene with the bride and groom

Author: Stella M. Reese

BY
CHARLOTTE

Printed in the United States
by Baker & Taylor Publisher Services